I REMEMBER

GEORGES PEREC

I REMEMBER

Introduced, Translated, Annotated, Edited & Indexed
by Philip Terry and David Bellos

A Verba Mundi Book
David R. Godine · Publisher · Boston

This is a Verba Mundi Book
published in 2014 by
DAVID R. GODINE, *Publisher*
Post Office Box 450
Jaffrey, New Hampshire 03452
www.godine.com

Library of Congress Cataloging-in-Publication Data

Perec, Georges, 1936–1982.
[Je me souviens. English]
I Remember / Georges Perec ; translated from the French by Philip
Terry, with an introduction and notes by David Bellos. – First edition.
p. cm. – "This is a Verba Mundi book."
Includes bibliographical references and index.
ISBN 978-1-56792-517-3 (alk. paper)
1. Perec, Georges, 1936–1982—Translations into English.
I. Terry, Philip, 1962– translator. II. Title.
PQ2676.E67J413 2014
848'.91409—dc23
2014004312

FIRST PRINTING
Printed in the United States of America

Contents

Introduction

GEORGES PEREC was born in Paris in 1936 to Polish immigrant parents. His father died in the defense of France in 1940; his mother was deported in 1943 and perished at Auschwitz. During the Occupation, Perec was cared for in the French Alps by his aunt and uncle, who brought him up in Paris after the end of the war. Around the age of eighteen he decided to be a writer. His first attempts at fiction, before and after his military service (1958-1960), met with the customary rejections, and in 1961 he took a job as a librarian in a medical research laboratory, which he kept until 1979. In 1965, however, he shot to fame as the author of a short, tight-lipped portrait of his own generation, *Things*. Not long after, he encountered the experimental writing group Oulipo, headed by Raymond Queneau and François le Lionnais. It changed him beyond recognition; Perec for his part transformed the group by becoming its most spectacularly successful and widely loved writer.

"Almost none of my books," Perec wrote in a famous short piece about himself for *Le Figaro* in 1978, "is entirely devoid of autobiographical traces ... likewise, almost none is assembled without recourse to one or another Oulipian structure or constraint, even if only symbolically, without the relevant constraint or structure constraining me in the least."*

I Remember is a striking example of such double ascendancy: it is manifestly autobiographical and also obeys

*Georges Perec, "Statement of Intent", in *Thoughts of Sorts*, 2009, p. 4.

a rigid (but not difficult) formal constraint. It is also one of the oddest works of literature ever written. Published in 1978 shortly after Perec's masterpiece, *Life A User's Manual*, won the Médicis Prize, *I Remember* is not a play, a poem, or a novel, and it's not a memoir in the ordinary sense either. It consists exclusively of sentences beginning "I remember…"—479 of them, plus an unfinished no. 480 consisting only of "I remember…"* Despite its unique and puzzling nature, however, *I Remember* quickly became one of France's most-loved short works. It has been imitated, parodied, reinvented, and adapted more than anything else Perec wrote. It's hardly possible to utter the words *"je me souviens…"* in French nowadays without committing a literary allusion.

Like many of Perec's projects, *I Remember* arose by happenstance. In 1970, Perec made the acquaintance of the American writer Harry Mathews. Harry, a tall and handsome expatriate, and the tousle-haired and barely solvent Parisian made a curious pair of bosom pals. Mathews was familiar with the New York art scene and told Perec about the serial autobiography that the painter Joe Brainard was bringing out, under the title *I Remember*, constructed exclusively of sentences beginning "I remember". It's not likely that Perec ever saw or read a copy of Brainard's work, but the idea of it appealed to him, and he made it his own. First he used it as a parlor game at the writer's retreat that he frequented, the Moulin d'Andé, in Normandy. The restrictions that Perec imposed for players of the game (which are not at all those used by Brainard) were that

*The addition of the blank no. 480, "I remember…" masks the fact that Perec's memory-list ends on the 42nd prime number.

you had to remember something that other people could remember too; and the thing remembered had to have ceased to exist. "I'd like to say 'I remember Vidal Sassoon,'" Perec complained, "but I can't, because he's still going." (However, that didn't stop him putting Vidal Sassoon, misspelled "Sasoon," in the published text.)

In the mid-1970s Perec started to use the "I remember" formula for a written exercise. He jotted down memories, mostly of his teenage years, in clutches, in 1973, 1975, and 1977. In 1976 he published a group of them in a periodical, and then decided to continue the routine until it made a whole book. As with many formally structured texts, the potential meaning of the work is partly a function of its length. A dozen "I remembers" might be just curious; a hundred of them could be irritating; beyond a certain point, however, a repeat-formula text creates new effects. It was Perec's peculiar genius to know how far he could go too far. The inventory of Mme Altamont's basement in Chapter 33 of *Life A User's Manual*, for example, exceeds all bounds of narrative relevance and common sense, but precisely because of its fantastical length it inspires exhilaration. Obstinate and unrelenting attempts at exhaustiveness provoke hilarity—and also a sense of the futility of all lists.

The "I remember" formula is eminently shareable. Anyone can write their own "I remembers": no special training or command of language is required, nor a jot of poetic or divine inspiration. It is therefore emblematic of the Oulipo's aim to invent tools for writing to be used by others. Perec requested his publishers to leave several blank pages at the end of each edition "for readers to write their own 'I remembers' which the reading of these ones will hopefully have inspired."

The formula has a personal function for Perec, whose other works are dotted with oblique and mostly invisible self-allusions. A memory entered here as something that Perec remembers may match exactly or else throw light on some tiny fragment you remember being mentioned somewhere else in his *œuvre*. *I Remember* allows the intensive reader of *Life A User's Manual* and other works to join things up, and to redraw the lines between fiction, memory, and history. Inevitably and no doubt intentionally, too, this book draws that other work into the field of autobiography. For example, why does François Breidel, the luckless husband of Mme de Beaumont's murdered daughter, pass through Château d'Oex (*Life A User's Manual*, p. 158)? See *I Remember*, no. 8. Why does Perec remember that Junot had been made Duc d'Abrantès (no. 20)? Because he must have spent some time gazing at the name-plate of the Avenue Junot (where the identity of Junot and Abrantès is explained) when writing the relevant sections of his *Places* project, involving repeated real-time descriptions of twelve different places in Paris, one of which was, precisely, Avenue Junot. Some of these links and echoes are mentioned in the notes at the end of the volume; readers may enjoy tracking down many others.

The restriction of "I remembers" to public or quasi-public facts and events has a significant consequence. The set of people who remember the Franco-Egyptian crooner Reda Caire performing at the Porte de Saint-Cloud cinema (no. 1) may or may not include members of the set of people who remember a Citroën 11CV with registration plate 7070RL2 (no. 2). Obviously, the small community established in the intersection of those two memory-groups automatically includes Georges Perec. Similarly, Perec belongs to the set of people who remember *Sixteen Tons* (no. 425), as I do, and to the set of those who remember that André Gide was mayor of a small town in Normandy (no. 222), which excludes me, but not a whole corporation of Gide scholars. In this way *I Remember* creates waves of partly overlapping sets of readers who share or do not share this or that memory, pushing each reader now closer to the center and now further away from it, but leaving one and only one inhabitant of the intersection of all 479 memories. That inhabitant is obviously Georges Perec, described, or rather, defined geometrically, in rich and intricate detail and in terms of his multiple relationships to groups and individuals among his contemporaries. When you stop to think, it's an amazing achievement, all the more so because it is done with the simplest of techniques. The "I remember" device using only shareable memories seems at first glance to dissolve the individual memoirist in a collective identify (that's to say, as a person who, just like thousands of others, remembers Garry Davis, or the capitulation of Japan), but in practice, when pursued far enough, it does quite the opposite: it locates the autobiographer in a 479-dimensional space in which his specific identity is made unique in a way than no amount of personal confession could achieve.

There is no known order or narrative logic to the memories that Perec listed in *I Remember*, and for that reason his formula harks back to many earlier uses of the "unordered list"—in ancient chronicles, for example, or in the famous chapter "The Year 1817" in *Les Misérables*, where Victor Hugo recites, higgledy-piggledy, over a hundred things he recalls from his youth. However, the addition of a repeated starting formula ("I remember …") and the numbering of the items turns "chaotic enumeration" into something more like a poem—that's to say, Perec's idea of a poem. The best example of this comes in *Life A User's Manual*, where he gives a catalog of the hand-tools marketed by Mme Moreau's home decorating business, culled from the actual catalogs of two French manufacturers (pp. 79–83). At the end of each catalog entry, Perec added "Fully guaranteed 1 yr." as a refrain; by his own account, that's what made his cut-and-paste catalog a poem.

I Remember has prompted more and less serious variations of the device by writers great and small, in works called *I Don't Remember...*, *I've Forgotten...* and so forth. However, the Canadian movie called *Je ne me souviens pas* ("I don't remember") owes its title not to Perec, but to the motto of the Province of Quebec, *Je me souviens*. Perec probably didn't remember it from his very short stay in Montreal, where he wrote the voice-over for an anthropological documentary whose material he adapted to construct the narrative of Chapter 25 of *Life A User's Manual*.

How good was Perec's memory? Not perfect. In the postscript on p. 97 below he himself gives the example of his own misremembering of the names of pre-war tennis stars. Other approximations and errors were pointed out by friends and readers after publication. "But it doesn't matter!" Perec is said to have riposted, "That's how *I* remember it!"* His purpose was not to give a documentary history of the popular culture of his teenage years, but to give an honest and authentic map of his *memory* of those years. In other words, the memory-field constituted by 479 frag-

*A Life in Words, pp. 636–637. For details of this and other books mentioned in the Introduction and Notes, see p. 17 below.

ments of a lost era is the autobiographical record of one part of the individual called Georges Perec as he was *in the 1970s*. Indeed, the only possible proofs of that assertion are the mistakes themselves. Readers can be forgiven for suspecting that the artful writer consciously inserted a couple of glitches to create exactly that effect—but even so, I'm sure that most of the mistakes Perec made are just mistakes.

The popularity of *I Remember* among Perec's French contemporaries (who are now in their late 70s) is one thing; its popularity among later generations is less easy to explain. Both owe something to the prominence of the classical *ubi sunt?* theme in European poetry, given memorable form by Villon's famous ballad of 1461, "Where are the snows of yesteryear?" (in Dante Gabriel Rossetti's nineteenth-century translation). The French original was set to a wistful tune by the guitarist-balladeer Georges Brassens in 1953, in an album called *Le Vent* ("The Wind"), and his tune was sung or at least hummed by an entire generation as the essence of agreeable nostalgia. (Other modern instances of the theme include Brecht and Weill's *Nanna's Lied*, and Pete Seeger's faux-folk version, *Where Have All the Flowers Gone?*, released as a single in 1964.) But in 1988, when the Avignon Festival honored Georges Perec with readings and an exhibition, Sami Frey performed *I Remember* on stage as a monologue, with a minimal set and a stationary bicycle as his only prop. It was a huge success, and was subsequently performed to packed houses for months on end at the Opéra-Comique and then the Mogador in Paris. It was revived in Paris in 2003 to even greater acclaim, made into a short movie, and has also toured the French provinces and Canada. The majority of the spectators of the show cannot conceivably share any of Perec's memories directly. The same must be true of the readership of this translation, few of whom could have been around in Paris in the period 1945–1965 (if they had been, they would most likely have read this work in French long ago).

The extended repetition of the formula "I remember," followed by what are now obscure and exotic names and events for French almost as much as for English readers, creates not nostalgia itself, but the impression, perhaps even the essence of nostalgia. By the peculiar magic of regulated repetition, the substantive content of Perec's "I remembers" gives way to a literary effect that is intensely pleasurable whilst being also desperately sad: not nostalgia itself (a longing for what has vanished and cannot be recovered), but the air, the mood, the sensation of nostalgia, over and above any substantive memories or regrets. What we now see in this strange book is not the resuscitation of the popular culture of a long-forgotten era, but a *human being* engaged in the effort of recapturing the popular culture of his youth. *I Remember*, like a *memento mori* of Renaissance art, is a poignant reminder of the vanity of all things. For we have indeed almost forgotten what it was like to be alive when we were young.

Perec knew what he was doing, but at the same time did his best to deny it. That's the reason for the excessive, manic, incomplete, and practically useless Index. An index of names and topics (the latter selected more by whim than reasoned design) gives *I Remember* the appearance of a work of historical reference, which it is not. Like the entirely useless Index of *La Boutique obscure* (Perec's *unpaginated* book of dream narratives) or the half-index of his spoof of the Algerian War, *Which Moped with Chrome-*

Plated Handlebars at the Back of the Yard?, which goes only
from A to P, the index of *I Remember* offers only a simu-
lation of order so as to plunge the reader into yet deeper
waters. What it offers is a re-jumbling of the unordered
material of the "I remembers" themselves. Alphabetical
order, because it is arbitrary with respect to content, makes
it clear that there is no natural or necessary order to memory. All Perec's indexes, including the huge and meticulous
index of *Life A User's Manual*, where fictional and historical characters are not distinguished from each other, are
anti-indexes. Secretly, also, they are angry pieces of work
in which the lowly research librarian uses his technical skill
to make plain not the neat orderliness, but the unending
messiness of life itself.

In 1986, the British novelist and *pasticheur* Gilbert
Adair (later to become the mind-bending translator of
Perec's *La Disparition*, in which the letter *e* is entirely
avoided) published his own imitation of *I Remember*.
It's not a translation, but a set of sentences all beginning
"I remember" that record memories of a British, not a
French childhood of the same period as Perec's. In this
new translation, Philip Terry has sought to reproduce
Perec's own memories of his adolescence, but now and
again he invents English stand-ins, especially for jokes
that play on the sounds and meanings of French words.
Perec invited his readers to add their own memories at the
back of this book; Terry's occasional modifications of the
original text, while not autobiographical in the way some
of my own notes are, can be thought of as gestures in the
same direction.

I Remember has prompted an admirable work of obses-
sive literary-cum-historical scholarship, Roland Brasseur's

Je me souviens de 'Je me souviens' ("I Remember *I Remember*," 1998) and its expanded edition, *Je me souviens encore mieux de 'Je me souviens'* ("I Remember Even More About *I Remember*," 2003). For each of Perec's "I remembers," Brasseur provides historical details and documentation, including reproductions of posters, advertising copy, cartoons, food labels … almost the entire two-dimensional universe of print and image that Perec's text alludes to. Brasseur would surely have included the sound of the jingles and songs had he started his project in the days of the e-book.

With Roland Brasseur's generous permission, I have raided his work for most of the information given in the Notes at the end of this book. Following his lead, dates of death have been added for many—alas, most—of the persons named in the Index, so that it bears the same historical relationship to 2013 as the original did to 1978. Philip Terry and I have also used some of the Index entries to add contextual information that makes some of the items less opaque for English readers. The Notes aren't intended to turn Perec's literary exercise into a historical document (despite the almost irresistible temptation to get to the bottom of every detail …), but to cast occasional rays of light on obscurities that readers could not easily pierce without knowledge of French or sets of multivolume encyclopedias to hand.

The most touching imitation of the formulaic design of *I Remember* is Harry Mathews's homage, *The Orchard*; the most despicable a column by Philippe Sollers in *Libération* ("I remember Georges Perec being dead drunk," and so on). But Perec's stupendously unpretentious work has also created a whole new *class* of constrained writing, called *textes à démarreur,* or "kick-starter texts." You are now licensed by Oulipo to write memoirs, fantasies, forecasts, confessions, narratives, or whatever grabs you in sets of numbered sentences beginning "I forgot …", or "I'm not the sort to …", or "I'm sorry that …", or "I know …", "Where did I read …?", "I wonder …" and so on. As the Oulipo's website states with characteristic and Perecquian generosity, *Tous les démarreurs sont autorisés,* "All kick-starters are allowed." On your marks, get set, go.

DAVID BELLOS
Princeton, NJ
August 2013

REFERENCES
Books mentioned in the Introduction and Footnotes

Gilbert Adair, *Myths and Memories.* London, Fontana, 1986
David Bellos, *Georges Perec: A Life in Words.* Boston, Godine, 1993
Roland Brasseur. *Je me souviens de 'Je me souviens'. Notes pour* Je me souviens *de Georges Perec à l'usage des générations oublieuses.* Paris, Le Castor Astral, 1998
Roland Brasseur, *Je me souviens encore mieux de 'Je me souviens'. Notes pour* Je me souvien*s de Georges Perec à l'usage des générations oublieuses.* Paris, Le Castor Astral, 2003
Frederick Forsyth, *The Day of the Jackal.* London, Hutchinson, 1971.
Romain Gary, *The Roots of Heaven* (1956), transl. Jonathan Griffin. London, White Lion, 1973
Victor Hugo, *The Wretched* (1862), transl. Christine Donougher. London, Penguin, 2013
Harry Mathews, *The Orchard: A Remembrance of Georges Perec.* Bamberger, 1998

Georges Perec, *Things* (1965), transl. David Bellos. In *Things: A Story of the Sixties & A Man Asleep*. Boston, Godine, 1990

Georges Perec, *Which Moped with Chrome-Plated Handlebars at the Back of the Yard?* (1966), transl. Ian Monk. In *Three By Perec*. Boston, Godine, 2004

Georges Perec, *A Man Asleep* (1967) transl. Andrew Leak. In *Things: A Story of the Sixties & A Man Asleep*. Boston, Godine, 1990

Georges Perec, *La Boutique Obscure* (1972), transl. Daniel Levin Becker. New York, Melville House, 2013

Georges Perec, *W or The Memory of Childhood* (1975), transl. David Bellos. Boston, Godine, 1988

Georges Perec, *An Attempt at Exhausting a Place in Paris*, transl. Marc Lowenthal. Cambridge, MA, Wakefield Press, 2010

Georges Perec, *Life A User's Manual* (1978), transl. David Bellos. New edition. Boston, Godine, 2009

Georges Perec, *Thoughts of Sorts* (1985), transl. David Bellos. Boston, Godine, 2009

Georges Perec, *"53 Days"* (1989). Edited by Harry Mathews and Jacques Roubaud, transl. David Bellos. Boston, Godine, 2002

Translator's Note

IN THE AFTERWORD to his translation of Perec's *An Attempt at Exhausting a Place in Paris*, Marc Lowenthal refers to *I Remember* as Perec's "most untranslatable book," describing it as "a collection of brief remembrances of things and people that are indecipherable to anyone not French and not of his generation" (p. 4). This doesn't explain why plenty of people neither of Perec's generation nor necessarily French *have* found this an immensely appealing book, but it does point to one of the major obstacles to translation: cultural reference. When I first talked to David Bellos about translating this text in 2011 and showed him my first drafts, he was encouraging, but quickly pointed out some of the mistakes I'd made because of gaps in my own cultural knowledge. He also pointed out other pitfalls: Perec's French is full of hidden puns and references and is never easy to translate—and if it looks easy, I should be especially wary. Some of Perec's "I remembers" that look fairly innocent, such as 88 and 194, turn out to conceal rebuses and mnemonics. Others consist of word games, extended puns, and jokes. These could only be "translated" by finding already existing English equivalents, or by creating something similar in English, starting from scratch. So Perec's memory no. 96:

> *Je me souviens de:*
> *"J'avais une soif de lionne:*
> *Voulant savoir à quoi l'eau sert,*
> *Je m'écriai: 'Tonnere! Avalons'".*

punning on place-names in the Department of Yonne (Auxerre, Avallon, Tonnerre), has acquired a different *literal* sense in English but still puns on place-names, now from Cornwall:

> I remember:
> Wondering where I'd put my new key
> I checked the loo,
> But found it in a mouse hole.

We battled away with these kinds of issues until we had only a few "impossibles" left, and eventually, some kind of a solution was found even for these, sometimes by means of a note. Throughout this long process David Bellos has provided suggestions, corrections, and reformulations, and while I did not agree with these in every case, he has left his mark one way or another on over a hundred of the entries. The translations of 78, 110, 121, 141, 220, 281, 336, 346, 377, and 475 owe their current form entirely to him. His input has made this translation much better than it would otherwise have been, and it has made me a slightly better, and much warier, translator.

PHILIP TERRY

I REMEMBER

for Harry Mathews

The title, the form, and, to a certain extent, the spirit of these texts are inspired by *I Remember* by Joe Brainard.

~ 1 ~

I remember Reda Caire performing live at the Porte de
Saint-Cloud cinema.

~ 2 ~

I remember that my uncle had an 11CV with the registration
number 7070 RL2.

~ 3 ~

I remember the cinema Les Agriculteurs, and the leather
armchairs at the Caméra, and the twin seats at the Panthéon.

~ 4 ~

I remember Lester Young at the Club Saint-Germain;
he wore a blue silk suit with a red silk lining.

~ 5 ~

I remember Ronconi, Brambilla, and Jésus Moujica, and
Zaaf, the perennial red lantern.

~ 6 ~

I remember that Art Tatum called a piece "Sweet Lorraine"
because he had been in Lorraine during the 1914–18 war.

~ 7 ~

I remember "clackers."

8

I remember a one-armed Englishman who beat everyone at ping-pong at Château d'Oex.

9

I remember *Ploum ploum tra la la.*

10

I remember that a friend of my cousin Henri spent all day in his dressing-gown when he was studying for his exams.

11

I remember the Citizen of the World Garry Davis tapping away on his typewriter on the Place du Trocadéro.

12

I remember games of *barbu* at Les Petites-Dalles.

13

I remember the Three Sees: Metz, Toul, and Verdun.

14

I remember the yellow bread there was for a while after the war.

15

I remember the earliest pinball machines, called *flippers* in French. But they didn't have any flippers.

∽ 16 ∼

I remember old issues of *L'Illustration*.

∽ 17 ∼

I remember the pick-up needles made of steel, and ones made of bamboo, which you had to sharpen on an abrasive strip after every record.

∽ 18 ∼

I remember that in Monopoly, Avenue de Breteuil is green, Avenue Henri Martin red, and Avenue Mozart orange.

∽ 19 ∼

I remember:

> Ich weiss nicht was soll es bedeuten
> Das Ich so traurig bin.

And:

> I wander lonely as a cloud
> When all at once I see a crowd
> A — ? — of golden daffodils.

∽ 20 ∼

I remember that Junot was duc d'Abrantès.

∽ 21 ∾

I remember:

Grégoire and Amédée
present
Grégoire and Amédée
in
Grégoire and Amédée
(and *Furax* too, of course).

∽ 22 ∾

I remember one day my cousin Henri visited a cigarette factory and brought back a cigarette as long as five normal ones.

∽ 23 ∾

I remember that after the war you almost never came across *chocolat viennois* or *chocolat liégois*, and that for a long time I got them mixed up.

∽ 24 ∾

I remember that the first L.P. I heard was the *Concerto for Woodwind and Orchestra* by Cimarosa.

∽ 25 ∾

I remember a school prefect from Corsica who was called Flack, "like German ack-ack."

∽ 26 ∾

I remember "High Life" and "Naja."

✎ 27 ✎

I remember getting an autograph from Louison Bobet at the Parc des Princes.

✎ 28 ✎

I remember that for a number of years, the dirtiest expression that I knew was *tremper la soupe*; I'd seen it in a dictionary of slang that I'd read in secret. I've never heard anyone actually use it and I'm no longer very sure what it means (no doubt a variant on "reaming").

✎ 29 ✎

I remember *Les Quatre Fils Aymon* and another tale called *Jean de Paris*.

✎ 30 ✎

I remember the Thursday afternoon screenings at the Royal-Passy cinema. There was one film called *Les Trois Desperados*, and another, *Les Cinq Balles d'Argent*, which ran for several episodes.

✎ 31 ✎

I remember that one of the first times I went to the theatre my cousin got the wrong playhouse – mixing up the Odéon and the Salle Richelieu – and instead of a classic tragedy, I saw *L'Inconnue d'Arras* by Armand Salacrou.

↜ 32 ↝

I remember that the real name of Lord Mountbatten was Battenberg.

↜ 33 ↝

I remember scarves made out of parachute silk.

↜ 34 ↝

I remember the cinema in Avenue de Messine.

↜ 35 ↝

I remember the Cerdan-Dauthuille match.

↜ 36 ↝

I remember that the city of Algiers stretches from Pointe Pescade to Cap Matifou.

↜ 37 ↝

I remember that at the end of the war, my cousin Henri and I marked the advance of the Allied armies with little flags bearing the names of the generals commanding the armies or the army corps. I've forgotten the names of almost all of these generals (Bradley, Patton, Zhukov, etc.) but I remember the name of General de Larminat.

↜ 38 ↝

I remember that Michel Legrand made his debut under the name of "Big Mike."

39

I remember that a 400-meter sprinter was caught stealing in the cloakrooms of a sports stadium (and that, to avoid going to prison, he had to sign up for Indochina).

40

I remember the day Japan capitulated.

41

I remember a piece by Earl Bostic that was called "Flamingo."

42

I remember that I used to wonder if the American actor William Bendix was the son of the washing machines.

43

I remember Albinoni's "Adagio."

44

I remember Jean Lec's radio program, *Le Grenier de Montmartre.*

45

I remember the satisfaction I felt when doing a Latin translation if I came across a whole sentence ready-made in Gaffiot.

◦ 46 ◦

I remember the period when the fashion was for black shirts.

◦ 47 ◦

I remember crystal radios.

◦ 48 ◦

I remember I started a collection of matchboxes and one of cigarette packets.

◦ 49 ◦

I remember that Edith Piaf was responsible for giving their first breaks to Les Compagnons de la Chanson, Eddie Constantine, and Yves Montand.

◦ 50 ◦

I remember the period when Sacha Distel was a jazz guitarist.

◦ 51 ◦

I remember the buses with a platform at the back: when you wanted to get off at the next stop, you had to press a buzzer, but neither too close to the preceding stop, nor too close to the stop in question.

◦ 52 ◦

I remember the time when a (ten-story) building that had just been completed at the bottom of Avenue de la Sœur-Rosalie was the tallest in Paris and passed for a skyscraper.

53

I remember I was very disappointed to learn that the actress Maggie McNamara only acted in *The Moon is Blue*. Later, I found that she was the daughter of the Secretary for Defense.

54

I remember that Voltaire is the anagram of "Arouet L(e) J(eune)," writing V instead of U and I instead of J.

55

I remember that Raoul Lévy went bankrupt trying to make a film spectacular called *Marco Polo*.

56

I remember that it was Sacha Guitry who came up with the slogan "Eleska's exquisite."

57

I remember that Christian Jaque divorced Renée Faure in order to marry Martine Carol.

58

I remember that the racing driver Sommer was nicknamed "the wild boar of the Ardennes."

59

I remember GARAP.

~ 60 ~

I remember G-7 taxis with glass partitions and jump seats.

~ 61 ~

I remember that Les Noctambules and Le Quartier Latin in Rue Champollion were theaters.

~ 62 ~

I remember scoubidous.

~ 63 ~

I remember "Dumpitty-dum, dumpitti-do, buy Dop Dop Dop Shampoo."

~ 64 ~

I remember how enjoyable it was, at boarding school, to be ill and to go to the sick room.

~ 65 ~

I remember that at the time of its launch, the weekly paper *Le Hérisson* ("*Le Hérisson* tickles you pink!") put on a big show during which, in particular, several boxing matches took place.

～ 66 ～

I remember an operetta featuring the Frères Jacques, and Irène Hilda, Jacques Pils, Armand Mestral and Maryse Martin. (There was another one, a few years later, also featuring the Frères Jacques, called *La Belle Arabelle*; it might have been in that one, and not in the first, that Armand Mestral appeared.)

～ 67 ～

I remember that I became, if not good, at least a little bit less hopeless in English, from the day I was the only one in the class to understand that "earthenware" meant *poterie*.

～ 68 ～

I remember when to get a new car you had to go on a waiting list for months, even a year or more.

～ 69 ～

I remember that at Villard-de-Lans I found it very funny that a refugee called Norman lived with a peasant called Breton. A few years later, in Paris, I laughed out loud when I heard that a restaurant called Le Lamartine was famous for its chateaubriands.

～ 70 ～

I remember the "True or False?", "Did You Know?", and "Strange but True" columns in children's comics.

✎ 71 ✎

I remember Jean Bretonnière when he sang *Toi ma p'tit' folie*.

✎ 72 ✎

I remember the live acts that used to take place at the Gaumont-Palace. I also remember the Gaumont-Palace.

✎ 73 ✎

I remember the difficulty they had digging out the foundations for the Drugstore Saint-Germain.

✎ 74 ✎

I remember the wooden man at the Galeries Barbès.

✎ 75 ✎

I remember *La Minute de Saint-Granier*.

✎ 76 ✎

I remember the motor-paced racing cyclists at the Parc des Princes.

✎ 77 ✎

I remember that Langres is famous for three things: its record low temperatures, its cutlery industry, and Diderot.

I remember the slogans used by two rival department stores: *Les yeux fermés, j'achète tout au Printemps* ("I can buy anything at *Le Printemps* with my eyes closed") and *Quand je les ouvre, j'achète au Louvre* ("When they're open, I shop at *Le Louvre*").

～ 79 ～

I remember "Ridgeway The Germ."

～ 80 ～

I remember Ray Ventura's big band.

～ 81 ～

I remember that one of the ski slopes at Villard-de-Lans is called "Les Clochettes," another "Les Bains," and the hardest of all "La Cote 2000."

～ 82 ～

I remember *Papa, Maman, la Bonne et Moi.*

～ 83 ～

I remember that one of the books that most set me dreaming was a treatise on etiquette with a preface by Baron André de Fouquières.

～ 84 ～

I remember that Michel Butor was born in Mons-en-Barœul.

85

I remember the Kravchenko affair.

86

I remember that Alain Delon was assistant pork butcher (or apprentice butcher?) in Montrouge.

87

I remember that *Caravan*, by Duke Ellington, was a rare disc and that, for years, I knew of its existence without having ever heard it.

88

I remember "*un soudard ne vit que de rapines obscures.*"

89

I remember that Jean Grémillon died on the same day as Gérard Philipe.

90

I remember the Capoulade and the Mahieu.

91

I remember a revue called *Je Sais Tout* for which the symbol was a man with a body in the form of the terrestrial globe (wasn't it rather a terrestrial globe metamorphosed into a face?).

❧ 92 ❧

I remember that "quatre quarts" owes its name to the fact it's made from a quarter milk, a quarter sugar, a quarter flour, and a quarter butter.

❧ 93 ❧

I remember "Pondichéry, Karikal, Mahé, Yanaon."

❧ 94 ❧

I remember when I was given detention.

❧ 95 ❧

I remember that in the film *Knock on Wood* Danny Kaye is mistaken for a spy called Gromeck.

❧ 96 ❧

I remember:

> Wondering where I'd put my new key
> I checked the loo,
> But found it in a mouse hole.

❧ 97 ❧

I remember that Monsieur Coudé du Foresto was the French delegate to the U.N. and that a pun was made on his name that I couldn't understand (it was, besides, very limp).

98

I remember that Shirley MacLaine made her debut in Hitchcock's *The Trouble with Harry.*

99

I remember that during the month of December a luxury food store in Avenue Mozart charged a small fortune for baskets of fruit featuring notoriously rare "Christmas raisins" that were ovoid, very plump, translucent, and tasteless.

100

I remember that Admiral Thierry d'Argenlieu was a monk.

101

I remember the "musketeers" of tennis: Petra, Borotra, Cochet, and Destremau.

102

I remember Xavier Cugat.

103

I remember "This is Cinerama."

104

I remember the Kovacs affair, still referred to as "the bazooka affair."

∽ 105 ∼

I remember "Bébé Cadum."

∽ 106 ∼

I remember that in September, in Paris, in the years after the war, there were lots of wasps, a lot more if you ask me than there are today.

∽ 107 ∼

I remember that performances of *La Petite Hutte* continued for several years and that this constituted a record.

∽ 108 ∼

I remember that *Fleur de Cactus* also had a very long run and that this enabled Sophie Desmarets to buy an antiques shop in the Passage Choiseul, which she called "Cactus Bazaar."

∽ 109 ∼

I remember the fashion for duffle-coats.

∽ 110 ∼

I remember Paul Ramadier and his goatee.

∽ 111 ∼

I remember when there were little blue buses with a flat fare.

✎ 112 ∾

I remember that Colette was a member of the Royal Academy of Belgium.

✎ 113 ∾

I remember an aperitif that was called "le Bonal."

✎ 114 ∾

I remember "Prosper youp-la-boum."

✎ 115 ∾

I remember the third-class carriages on trains.

✎ 116 ∾

I remember that in *Merrily We Live*, there are two dogs, one called "Get out of it," the other "You too."

✎ 117 ∾

I remember that Jean Gabin, before the war, had a contract stipulating that he had to die at the end of each film.

✎ 118 ∾

I remember the Yves Klein exhibition, at the Gallery Allendy, Rue de l'Assomption.

✎ 119 ∾

I remember that it took several days for René Coty to be elected President of the Republic at Versailles.

120

I remember the two films of Roberto Benzi.

121

I remember "Astra" margarine: "… why waste your money on anything else?…"

122

I remember that Agnès Varda was a photographer at the Théâtre National Populaire.

123

I remember that the violinist Ginette Neveu died in the same plane as Marcel Cerdan.

124

I remember the Andréa Doria.

125

I remember that Khrushchev hit his desk with his shoe at the UN.

126

I remember when *l'Express* became a daily paper.

127

I remember Walkowiak.

∾ 128 ∾

I remember that Jeanne Moreau acted at the Théâtre National Populaire.

∾ 129 ∾

I remember that at Michel-Ange–Auteuil, where today there is a Monoprix (or a Prisunic), there used to be a cinema.

∾ 130 ∾

I remember that Poirot-Delpech was the court reporter at *Le Monde*.

∾ 131 ∾

I remember the Kon-Tiki Expedition.

∾ 132 ∾

I remember my astonishment the day I found out that the Palais de Chaillot had nothing to do with the Trocadéro.

∾ 133 ∾

I remember that my first bicycle had solid tires.

∾ 134 ∾

I remember that two of the Frères Jacques really are brothers and that they are called Bellec, like one of my old classmates.

I remember that Henri Salvador recorded something like the first French Rock and Roll records under the name Henry Cording.

~ 136 ~

I remember when we came back from holiday, on the first of September, and there was still a whole month without school.

~ 137 ~

I remember the kidnapping of the Peugeot boy.

~ 138 ~

I remember that Jean Bobet – the brother of Louison – had a degree in English.

~ 139 ~

I remember the concert presenter Charles Bassompierre.

~ 140 ~

I remember:

> "We are ze lads from ze navy,
> from China to France to Chile,
> from ze littl' uns to ze big 'uns,
> from ze ship's boys to ze captains,
> people greet uz wiz eyes agogs,
> the garlic crunching sea dogs."

∽ 141 ∾

I remember that at the bottom of the footbridge near the top of Rue du Ranelagh that crossed the Ceinture railroad line and led to the Bois de Boulogne, there was a little shack which served as a shoemaker's workshop, and that, after the war, it was covered in swastikas because the shoemaker had been a collaborator, or so people said.

∽ 142 ∾

I remember that Alain Robbe-Grillet was an agronomist.

∽ 143 ∾

I remember that I used to think that the first bottles of Coca-Cola – those which American soldiers would have drunk during the war – contained Benzedrine (which I was very proud to know was the scientific name of "Maxiton").

∽ 144 ∾

I remember that I didn't like sauerkraut.

∽ 145 ∾

I remember that I adored the film *Bathing Beauty* with Esther Williams and Red Skelton, but was terribly disappointed when I saw it again.

∽ 146 ∾

I remember how shit scared I was – as a boarder – that they'd cover my dick with shoe polish.

~ 147 ~

I remember that Avenue de New York used to be called Avenue de Tokyo.

~ 148 ~

I remember that Fidel Castro was a barrister.

~ 149 ~

I remember Charles Rigoulot.

~ 150 ~

I remember I was astonished to learn that my first name meant "worker of the soil."

~ 151 ~

I remember that it was because of the seed shops that François Truffaut, when he was in the army, wrote a series of letters to Louise de Vilmorin which were subsequently published in the weekly *Arts*.

~ 152 ~

I remember that Warren Beatty is the younger brother of Shirley MacLaine.

~ 153 ~

I remember that in third year I spent more than two weeks making a huge map of Ancient Rome.

∾ 154 ∾

I remember that Paderewski was elected President of the Polish Republic.

∾ 155 ∾

I remember the first demonstration I took part in was over the appointment – or the return – to the Sorbonne of the *Pétainiste* Jean Guitton.

∾ 156 ∾

I remember Henri Kubnick's broadcasts.

∾ 157 ∾

I remember that Darry Cowl's real name is André Darrigaud.

∾ 158 ∾

And that reminds me of the cyclist André Darrigade.

∾ 159 ∾

I remember that Maurice Ravel was very proud of the popularity of his *Boléro*.

∾ 160 ∾

I remember that racing cyclists used to carry an emergency inner tube rolled into a figure eight wrapped round their shoulders.

∽ 161 ∾

I remember that Claudia Cardinale was born in Tunis
(or in any case in Tunisia).

∽ 162 ∾

I remember that I was proud to know and use, relatively
early, words and expressions like "here come the cavalry,"
"runner," "caduceus," "at the crack of dawn."

∽ 163 ∾

I remember that, in the carriages of the métro, the map of
the line showed, in a box beneath the name of each station,
the roads and the numbers of the roads on which the exits
opened (how to put that more simply?).

∽ 164 ∾

I remember that Carette died because he was wearing a
nylon shirt and he dropped off to sleep smoking a cigarette.

∽ 165 ∾

I remember that after the death of Martine Carol,
somebody broke into her grave hoping to find valuable
jewelry, or so people surmised.

∽ 166 ∾

I remember that Dinu Lipatti learned to play the piano very
late, around the age of twenty.

∽ 167 ∾

I remember that The Platters were involved in a drug scandal, and also that it was rumored that Dalida was an agent for the FLN.

∽ 168 ∾

I remember the six-day events at the Vél d'Hiv.

∽ 169 ∾

I remember the concerts organized by Norman Granz called "Jazz at the Philharmonic."

∽ 170 ∾

I remember the theaters Les Deux-Anes and Les Trois-Baudets.

∽ 171 ∾

I remember the ballets of the Marquis de Cuevas.

∽ 172 ∾

I remember that Dr. Spock ran for President of the United States.

∽ 173 ∾

I remember Jacqueline Auriol, "the fastest woman in the world."

174

I remember May '68.

175

I remember Biafra.

176

I remember the war between India and Pakistan.

177

I remember Yuri Gagarin.

178

I remember that the Studio Jean Cocteau was formerly called the Celtic.

179

I remember that the day after the death of Gide, Mauriac received a telegram saying "Hell doesn't exist. Enjoy yourself. Stop. Gide."

180

I remember that Burt Lancaster used to be an acrobat.

181

I remember that Johnny Halliday made an appearance as a special guest star at Bobino supporting Raymond Devos (I think I even said something along the lines of: "if this guy makes it I'm going to top myself...").

〜 182 〜

I remember that Marina Vlady made her debut in a film by Cayatte called *Après Nous le Déluge*.

〜 183 〜

I remember that I was often confused with a pupil called Bellec.

〜 184 〜

I remember that I used to have a torch with a handle which made it look like a revolver.

〜 185 〜

I remember the holes that used to be punched in métro tickets.

〜 186 〜

I remember Bonino's one-man-show.

〜 187 〜

I remember that the trumpet player Clifford Brown died at age twenty in a car crash.

〜 188 〜

I remember the Colgate adverts with Geneviève Cluny, *Miss White-Teeth*.

✑ 189 ✑

I remember that SFIO stood for "French Section of the Socialist International."

✑ 190 ✑

I remember the jazz broadcasts presented by Sim Copans.

✑ 191 ✑

I remember the surprise I felt when I learned that *cowboy* meant "cattle herder."

✑ 192 ✑

I remember the racing cyclist Louis Caput.

✑ 193 ✑

I remember that Robespierre had his jaw broken by the soldier Merda, who later became a colonel.

✑ 194 ✑

I remember:

> "Say it, eh Shaun, pronounced the whale, I've a dull fin, but don't lack purpose."

and

> "Keats mines Wordsworth's coal ridge."

✑ 195 ✑

I remember radio talent shows.

～ 196 ～

I remember that Marina Vlady is the sister of Odile Versois
(and that they're the daughters of the painter Poliakoff).

～ 197 ～

I remember the films featuring the dog Rin-Tin-Tin, and
also those featuring Shirley Temple, and also the poems of
Minou Drouet.

～ 198 ～

I remember the thirteen-a-side rugby champion Puig-
Aubert, nicknamed "Pipette."

～ 199 ～

I remember the "*Ballets roses*" scandal involving the
Speaker of the French parliament, André Le Troquer.

～ 200 ～

I remember that at the Bûcherie café, before it was
expanded, there used to be a tapestry by Jean Lurçat on
which you could read the following verse: "Night hides
day on the other side of dark."

～ 201 ～

I remember that where there's now a Hippopotamus
(on the left bank, not far from Maubert) there used to
be a restaurant run by the famous chef Garin.

I remember the fashion for knitted silk ties.

I remember that the métro station Charles-Michels (and, I suppose, Place Charles-Michels) used to be called "Beaugrenelle."

I remember the song "La petite diligence," and one that began "Basil, where are you going to on your white horse?" and another that went "I haven't killed, I haven't robbed, but I didn't believe my mother."

I remember the newspaper containing Chaban-Delmas's tax returns.

I remember that the first name of all Pierre Benoit's heroines began with the letter A (I never understood why this was considered remarkable).

I remember that Sophie always won races against Pierre and Charles, because Charles *traînait* and Pierre *freinait*, whereas Sophie *démarrait* – Charles dawdled, Pierre braked, and Sophie took off.

⤖ 208 ⤗

I remember *Les Lettres Françaises.*

⤖ 209 ⤗

I remember that in *The Jungle Book*, Bagheera is the panther, Mowgli the boy, and Bandar Log the monkey (but what are the names of the bear and the snake?).

⤖ 210 ⤗

I remember that Fausto Coppi had a lady-friend called "The Woman in White."

⤖ 211 ⤗

I remember a cheese called "La Vache sérieuse" ("La Vache qui rit" took the manufacturers to court and won).

⤖ 212 ⤗

I remember a Mexican comic actor called Cantinflas (I think he was the one who played Passepartout in *Around the World in Eighty Days*).

⤖ 213 ⤗

I remember the swimmer Alex Jany.

⤖ 214 ⤗

I remember Jacques Duclos' pigeons.

∽ 215 ∾

I remember that Jean-Paul Sartre worked on the script of ⎤
John Huston's *Freud*. ⎦

∽ 216 ∾

I remember that I learned with great care the names of the
colors in heraldry: "sinople" means green, "sable" black,
"gules" red, etc.

∽ 217 ∾

I remember the "mere handful" of generals behind the
Algiers Putsch: Salan, Jouhaud, Challe, and Zeller.

∽ 218 ∾

I remember:

> "Jules plays Hector, Séraphin's a musician, mum's a
> sleepwalker, and I'm decommissioned."

And:

> "There's nine teen eighty-four
> There's eight and love
> There's seven and hell
> There's six and marriage
> There's five ours and graces
> There's four in travel
> There's three trees and declarations
> There's two testaments, the old and the new,
> But there's only one hair on Matthew's head
> And there's only one tooth in Saint John's"

I remember "Carter" liver salts.

I remember people saying that Bernard Buffet was so poor and so obsessed with painting that all he had to paint on were his own sheets!

I remember the cartoons by Sennep in *Le Figaro* and those by Mittelberg (who later used the name Tim) in *L'Humanité*.

I remember that André Gide was the mayor of a little village in Normandy, and that he claimed to be a pomologist.

I remember the record sleeves, mostly for jazz, designed by David Stone Martin.

I remember that the first film in Cinemascope was called *The Robe* (and that it was rubbish).

I remember that Boris Vian died while coming out of a showing of a film adapted from his book *I Spit on Your Graves*.

∽ 226 ∾

I remember Pils and Tabet.

∽ 227 ∾

I remember that the cyclist Ferdinand (Ferdi) Kubler carried his sunglasses (in mica with an elastic headband) above the bend of the elbow, like a ski champion, whereas other cyclists tended to wear them on their foreheads or over the visors of their helmets.

∽ 228 ∾

I remember Dario Moreno.

∽ 229 ∾

I remember that Roger Vailland wrote a play called *Le Colonel Foster plaidera coupable* that was banned by the Minister of the Interior.

∽ 230 ∾

I remember that at the end of the war, there was a "Petiot affair" which resembled the Landru affair.

∽ 231 ∾

I remember the program by Harris and Sedouy, *Seize millions de jeunes.*

∽ 232 ∾

I remember the Russian clown Popov, and the Swiss clown Grock.

✑ 233 ✑

I remember several footballers: Ben Barek, Marche and Jonquet, and, later, Just Fontaine.

✑ 234 ✑

I remember that toward the middle of the 1950s it was the fashion for a while to wear in place of a tie little laces that were almost indescribably narrow.

✑ 235 ✑

I remember the saxophonist Barney Willem.

✑ 236 ✑

I remember that the palindrome of Horace – Ecaroh – is the title of a piece by Horace Silver.

✑ 237 ✑

I remember the fire at the Drugstore des Champs-Élysées.

✑ 238 ✑

I remember Sabu.

✑ 239 ✑

I remember Malcolm X.

✑ 240 ✑

I remember that the first métro line to run on tires was Châtelet–Lilas.

∽ 241 ∽

I remember Doctor Bombard.

∽ 242 ∽

I remember that during the war the English had Spitfires and the Germans Stukas (and Messerchmitts).

∽ 243 ∽

I remember the Declaration of the 121.

∽ 244 ∽

I remember that Stendhal liked spinach.

∽ 245 ∽

I remember the Lépine Contest.

∽ 246 ∽

I remember that Citroën used the Eiffel Tower for a gigantic illuminated advertisement.

∽ 247 ∽

I remember that de Gaulle had a brother called Pierre who ran the Foire de Paris.

∽ 248 ∽

I remember the Finaly affair.

❧ 249 ❧

I remember the young actor Robert Lynen, who appeared in *Poil de Carotte* and in *Carnet de bal* (in which he had a very small part) and who died at the beginning of the war.

❧ 250 ❧

I remember the assassination attempt at Petit-Clamart.

❧ 251 ❧

I remember the cinema Le Studio Universel in Avenue de l'Opera, which specialized in animation festivals.

❧ 252 ❧

I remember that Lester Young was nicknamed "The Prez" and Paul Quinichette "The Vice-Prez."

❧ 253 ❧

I remember that SHAPE stood for the Supreme Headquarters Allied Powers Europe.

❧ 254 ❧

I remember Bouvard and Ratinet log tables.

❧ 255 ❧

I remember the murder of Sharon Tate.

✑ 256 ✑

I remember that the principal victims of McCarthyism in the world of cinema were the filmmakers Cyril Entfield, John Berry, Jules Dassin, and Joseph Losey, as well as the script-writer Dalton Trumbo. All of them went into exile, except Dalton Trumbo, who was obliged to work under assumed names for several years.

✑ 257 ✑

I remember that Audie Murphy was the most decorated American soldier of the Second World War and that he became an actor after having played himself in a (mediocre) film recounting his heroic exploits.

✑ 258 ✑

I remember that James Stewart played the part of Glenn Miller in the biopic of this jazz musician whose most famous piece is "Moonlight Serenade."

✑ 259 ✑

I remember that one of the first decisions that de Gaulle took on coming to power was to abolish the belt worn with jackets in the military.

✑ 260 ✑

I remember that the four sentences written on the pediments of the Palais de Chaillot were composed specially by Paul Valéry.

✐ 261 ∾

I remember that once the counter and the kitchen area of the restaurant La Petite Source in Boulevard Saint-Germain were situated on the right of the entrance and not, as now, on the left in the back.

✐ 262 ∾

I remember that Julien Gracq was a history teacher at Lycée Claude-Bernard.

✐ 263 ∾

I remember President Rosko.

✐ 264 ∾

I remember a dance called the raspa.

✐ 265 ∾

I remember Lee Harvey Oswald.

✐ 266 ∾

I remember beard tennis: you counted the number of beards you spotted in the street: 15 for the first, 30 for the second, 40 for the third, and "game" for the fourth.

267 ~

I remember the song:

    "Ramadjah my Queen
    Ramadjah my clot
    Dip your arse in the soup tureen
    And tell me if it's hot."

268 ~

I remember that during his trial Eichmann was enclosed in a glass cage.

269 ~

I remember the boxer Ray Famechon, as well as Stock and Charron, and quite a few wrestlers (The White Angel, The Béthune Butcher, The Little Prince, Doctor Adolf Kaiser, etc.).

270 ~

I remember the Markowitch Affair.

271 ~

I remember the strips of mica or celluloid that people used to fix on the front of their hoods (near the radiator cap) and which stopped mosquitoes and aphids from hitting the windscreen.

272 ~

I remember that the three star dancers of the Paris Ballet were Roland Petit, Jean Guélais, and Jean Babilée.

～ 273 ～

I remember that Saint Crispin and Saint Crispinian are the
patron saints of shoe-makers.

～ 274 ～

I remember a very beautiful recital given in Chartres
Cathedral (in 1953?) by the pianist Monique de la
Bruchollerie.

～ 275 ～

I remember an anecdote that traced the invention of
mayonnaise back to the siege of Port-Mahon (under
Napoleon III).

～ 276 ～

I remember that Jean Jaurès was assassinated at the Café du
Croissant in Rue Montmartre.

～ 277 ～

I remember oil slicks (the first, the Torrey-Canyon) and red
mud.

～ 278 ～

I remember that the word *robot* is a Czech word, invented,
I think, by Carel Capek.

～ 279 ～

I remember the adventures of Luc Bradfer.

I remember Woody Herman's big band.

I remember that the ranks of *caporal* and *sergent* in the French infantry are called *brigadier* and *maréchal-des-logis* in the artillery, the tank corps, and logistics.

I remember that Maurice Chevalier had a property at Marnes-la-Coquette.

I remember the plastic explosives planted towards the end of the Algerian War, and that a tailor on Boulevard Saint-Germain, Jack Romoli, was targeted several times.

I remember the three heroines in *Girls* by George Cukor: Taina Egg (a Finn), Mitzi Gaynor, and the wife of Rex Harrison, Kay Kendall, who died shortly after making the film.

I remember that all the numbers whose digits add up to nine are divisible by nine (sometimes I spent whole afternoons checking that it was true ...).

I remember the time it was rare to see trousers without turn-ups.

I remember Porfirio Rubirosa (the son-in-law of Trujillo?).

I remember that "Caran d'Ache" is a Frenchified transcription of a Russian word (Karandash?) which means "pencil."

I remember the two cabarets in the Contrescarpe district: Le Cheval d'Or and Le Cheval Vert.

I remember "Chérie je t'aime, chérie je t'adore" (also known as "Moustapha") in a version by Bob Azzam and his orchestra.

I remember that the first film I saw with Jerry Lewis and Dean Martin was called *Sailor Beware*.

∽ 292 ∾

I remember the hours I spent, in third year I think, trying
to provide a supply of water, gas, and electricity to three
houses without the pipes crossing (a solution isn't possible
so long as you remain in a two-dimensional plane; it's
an example of elementary topology, like the bridges of
Königsberg, or the coloring of maps).

∽ 293 ∾

I remember:

> Should you say "There is only two ways of poaching
> an egg" or "There are only two ways of poaching an
> egg"?

And:

> What color was Henri IV's white horse?

∽ 294 ∾

I remember that the central character in *The Outsider*
is called Antoine (?) Meursault: it's often been said that
nobody remembers his name.

∽ 295 ∾

I remember candy-floss at fairgrounds.

∽ 296 ∾

I remember the lipstick "Kiss," "the lipstick that doesn't
stop you kissing".

∽ 297 ∾

I remember the marbles made out of clay that broke in two when you hit them too hard, and ones made out of agate, and the huge glass ones which sometimes had bubbles inside.

∽ 298 ∾

I remember the front-wheel-drive gang.

∽ 299 ∾

I remember the Bay of Pigs.

∽ 300 ∾

I remember the Three Stooges, and Bud Abbott and Lou Costello; and Bob Hope, Dorothy Lamour, and Bing Crosby; and Red Skelton.

∽ 301 ∾

I remember that Sidney Bechet wrote an opera – or was it a ballet? – called *La nuit est une sorcière*.

∽ 302 ∾

I remember Hermès handbags, with their tiny padlocks.

∽ 303 ∾

I remember the difficulty I had understanding the meaning of the expression: "without solution of continuity."

I remember the game "Enrich your vocabulary" in *Reader's Digest*.

I remember "Burma" jewelry (and wasn't there also a jeweler called "Murat"?).

I remember:

> "Monday morning
> The Emperor, his wife, and the Little Prince
> Came round mine
> To make my acquaintance
> As I'd already gone out
> The Little Prince began to shout:
> Since he's gone away, we'll come back Tuesday."
> Etc.

I remember:

> – Why do musicians always get up late?
> – Because of the Partita 4 in D Flat.

I remember the question: "'Nebuchadnezzar,' how do you spell it?" and the answer: "i, t."

I remember: "My bells are jingling in my punts."

I remember:

> – What's the difference between a drunk, an
>   oversexed somnambulist, and my family?
> – ?
> – One of them slumps in a heap and the other humps
>   in his sleep.
> – What about your family?
> – They're all fine, thank you.

I remember Master Bates, Ben Dover, Seaman Staines,
and Roger the Cabin Boy.

I remember that Jean-Paul Sartre wrote a series of articles
about Cuba in *France-Soir* called *Ouragan sur le sucre*.

I remember Bourvil.

I remember a sketch by Bourvil in which he repeated
several times, at the end of each paragraph of his comic
lecture: "Alcohol, no, mineral water, yes!"

I remember, too, some of the films he made, *Pas si bête*,
and *Le Rosier de Madame Husson*.

I remember Wakouwas.

I remember that there was a battleship called the Georges Leygues.

I remember that I was very proud to know a lot of words derived from *caput*: captain, cap, chef, cattle, capital, capitol, capitulate, capstone, etc.

I remember *Wee Willie Winkie*, with Shirley Temple.

I remember Roger Nicolas, whose catchphrase was "Listen! Listen!"

I remember "Carambar."

I remember "Doctor Gustin's Lithium Salts."

I remember the month of May at Étampes, when we started going to the swimming pool.

✑ 322 ✑

I remember that I dreamed of one day having all 57 varieties of Heinz.

✑ 323 ✑

I remember Closterman and Commandant Mouchotte, who has since become for me the name of a cat that some friends found in Rue du Commandant-Mouchotte, at the back of Montparnasse.

✑ 324 ✑

I remember *First on the Rope* by Frison-Roche.

✑ 325 ✑

I remember the massive power-cut that plunged New York into darkness for several hours.

✑ 326 ✑

I remember Brigitte Fossey and Georges Poujouly in *Les Jeux interdits*.

✑ 327 ✑

I remember Théo Sarapo.

✑ 328 ✑

I remember a weekly that was called *Le Nouveau Candide*.

∽ 329 ∼

I remember that in *No Exit* there's a mystery surrounding a "bronze by Barbedienne."

∽ 330 ∼

I remember that I tried several times to use a slide-rule, and also repeatedly started on manuals of modern math, telling myself that if I took it slowly, if I read all the lessons in order, did the exercises and everything, then there was no reason for me to lose the thread.

∽ 331 ∼

I remember the Théâtre de Lutèce in Rue de Jussieu.

∽ 332 ∼

I remember La Cigale, at Pigalle, where Al Lirvat and his orchestra played for over thirty years.

∽ 333 ∼

I remember the Baader Meinhof gang.

∽ 334 ∼

I remember the New Wave.

∽ 335 ∼

I remember that in a New Wave short called *Histoire d'eau* Jean-Claude Brialy came out with this grandiose phrase: "The more I pedal slowly, the less I go fast."

✎ 336 ✎

I remember that when a news magazine declared itself to be "the journal of the New Wave" a satirical weekly objected that there must be better uses for hair gel.)

✎ 337 ✎

I remember Joseph Laniel.

✎ 338 ✎

I remember "Watch the beef."

✎ 339 ✎

I remember the radio programs (*Comme il vous plaira*) presented by Jean-Pierre Morphée and ?

✎ 340 ✎

I remember Jean Nohain, known as Jaboune, and his broadcast *Quarante millions de Français* (and *Reine d'un Jour?*).

✎ 341 ✎

I remember Jean Constantin when he sang "Où sont passées mes pantoufles?"

✎ 342 ✎

I remember Moustache.

✑ 343 ✑

I remember a jazz musician who was called Mowgli Jospin.

✑ 344 ✑

I remember the Golf Drouot night-club (I never went there).

✑ 345 ✑

I remember that *Signé Furax* and several other comedy broadcasts were produced by Pierre Arnaud de Chassis-Poulet.

✑ 346 ✑

I remember the ad for Wonder batteries: "They never wear out if you don't switch them on."

✑ 347 ✑

I remember *Carioca, Jumbo, Bambi*, and *The Three Caballeros* (and *Fantasia* of course).

✑ 348 ✑

I remember a book that was called *The Yearling*, and another that told the story of a beaver farmer (also involving an animal, some kind of stag, that I always called a "mouse" instead of a "moose"), and *My Friend Flicka*, and Mazo de la Roche.

✑ 349 ✑

I remember *Sur le banc*, with Raymond Souplex and Jane Sourza.

∽ 350 ∾

I remember the "Tracker" series of books (*La Bande des Ayacks*, *Le Prince Eric*, *Le Bracelet de vermeil*, etc.)

∽ 351 ∾

I remember Marie Besnard, the good woman of Loudun.

∽ 352 ∾

I remember: "With a waterproof made by C.C.C., the rain may knock but you hold the key" (at school, we said rather "and gets in scot-free").

∽ 353 ∾

I remember that the three magi were called Gaspard, Melchior, and Balthazar.

∽ 354 ∾

I remember that one of the Three Little Pigs is called Naf-Naf, but what about the others?

∽ 355 ∾

I only remember a few of the seven dwarfs: Grumpy, Dopey, Doc.

∽ 356 ∾

I remember a newspaper called *Radar*.

∽ 357 ∾

I remember "Émail Diamant" toothpaste with its singing toreador.

∽ 358 ∾

I remember the métro line Invalides–Porte de Vanves. It was the shortest in the whole of Paris. And now it forms a section of the longest.

∽ 359 ∾

I remember that my uncle had a device for sharpening his razor blades.

∽ 360 ∾

I remember a prefect at Lycée Claude-Bernard who had a yellow scarf; it was at this time that I learned that yellow was the color of cuckolds.

∽ 361 ∾

I remember when I found out that Köchel (pronounced *Queue-Chelle*) was a man and what the initials BWV meant.

∽ 362 ∾

I remember "worst things" jokes:

– What's the worst thing when it comes to fear?
– To recoil in front of the moving hands of a clock.
– What's the worst thing for a hairdresser?
– To cut his losses before he shaves a fortune.

363

I remember the film by Louis Daquin, *L'École buissonnière*, with Bertrand Blier, inspired by the Freinet method.

364

I remember that I belonged to a Book Club and that the first book I purchased was *Planus* by Cendrars.

365

I remember the advertisements painted on the sides of houses.

366

I remember the Soissons vase.

367

I remember Isettas, and also the fashion for scooters.

368

I remember the film *One Summer of Happiness*.

369

I remember Caryl Chessman.

370

I remember Abbé Pierre.

371

I remember myxomatosis.

372

I remember *The Lost Continent.*

373

I remember Zappy Max.

374

I remember Zatopek.

375

I remember the kidnapping of Fangio (by Castrists?).

376

I remember *Mister Magoo.*

377

I remember when cars honked, and the horns that went "quack-quack."

378

I remember the Goitschel sisters.

379

I remember the Caméléon jazz club in Rue Saint-André des Arts, with a drummer called Al Levitt.

380

I remember Bao Daï and, much later, Madame Nhu.

381

I remember the English racing cyclist Harris who held
the world record (for one hundred meters? for speed?)
on track.

382

I remember Picasso's dove, and his portrait of Stalin.

383

I remember Jean Paul David.

384

I remember: "When parents drink, children tipple."

385

I remember Cardinal Spellman.

386

I remember Group Captain Townsend.

387

I remember the Orinoco expedition. And Annapurna,
the first eight thousand meter ascent. And Sherpa Tensing.

388

I remember *Mr. Orchid*, with Noël-Noël.

~ 389 ~

I remember Christine Keeler and the Profumo Affair.

~ 390 ~

I remember Atlas the Giant (and the dwarf Pierhal?).

~ 391 ~

I remember Lumumba.

~ 392 ~

I remember that at the top of the Boulevard Saint-Michel there was a record shop called *Chanteclair,* I think, where, for the sum of twenty (old) francs, you could listen to a record (78 rpm).

~ 393 ~

I remember when I broke my arm and had the plaster cast signed by the whole class.

~ 394 ~

I remember sack races.

~ 395 ~

I remember "melts in the mouth, not in the hand."

∽ 396 ∾

I remember the reviews *Cahiers des Saisons, 84, Contemporains, Mercure de France, Table Ronde, Cahiers de la Pleiade,* etc., etc., etc.

∽ 397 ∾

I remember the Concert Pacra. And L'Européen.

∽ 398 ∾

I remember Vidal Sassoon.

∽ 399 ∾

I remember the "Provos."

∽ 400 ∾

I remember when I used to wait for the bell to ring at the end of class.

∽ 401 ∾

I remember an article by Claude Lanzmann in *Les Temps Modernes* called "From Smoked Herring to Caviar, or Passion According to Françoise Giroud."

∽ 402 ∾

I remember when liquorice powder was sold in little boxes that dissolved on the tongue.

~ 403 ~

I remember that Louis Malle began his career by filming *The Silent World* with Jacques Cousteau.

~ 404 ~

I remember Claude Luter at the Club Lorientais.

~ 405 ~

I remember the cabarets La Rose Rouge and La Fontaine des Quatre-Saisons.

~ 406 ~

I remember Paul-Émile Victor. And Haroun Tazieff.

~ 407 ~

I remember:

> – *Ouk Elabon´ Polin´?*
> – *Alagar, elpis éfé kaka!*

And:

> *Cesarem legato alacrem eorum.*

~ 408 ~

I remember the Liège–Bastogne–Liège cycle race, and Bordeaux–Paris, and Paris–Brest–Paris, and Paris–Camembert, and Milan–San Remo, and the Tour du Dauphiné, etc., etc., etc.

～ 409 ～

I remember the street processions after the *bac.*

～ 410 ～

I remember the old Montparnasse station.

～ 411 ～

I remember that there were two questions in the 1946
referendum and that my uncle explained that NO-YES
wasn't at all the same answer as YES-NO.

～ 412 ～

I remember Jacques Goddet and Georges Briquet.

～ 413 ～

I remember the Thursday radio program *Les Jeunes
Français sont musiciens.*

～ 414 ～

I remember a brand of petrol with a winged horse for a
symbol, and another called "Azur."

～ 415 ～

I remember pillow fights.

✑ 416 ~

I remember that the numbers of Peugeot models (201, 203, 302, 303, 403, 404, etc.) had a precise meaning, and also the numbers of trains (for example, Pacific 231).

✑ 417 ~

I remember *The Little King* by Otto Soglow, and the magazines I used to read waiting my turn at the hairdresser's.

✑ 418 ~

I remember the Renault Juvaquatre.

✑ 419 ~

I remember the baths I used to take on Saturday afternoons after coming back from school.

✑ 420 ~

I remember that I used to dream of getting Meccano n° 6.

✑ 421 ~

I remember the lead soldiers that were really made of lead, and clay soldiers.

✑ 422 ~

I remember when I was a Cub Scout, but I've forgotten the name of my Pack.

I remember the luminous adverts during the intermission at the *Royal-Passy* cinema.

I remember:

> "How much is that doggy in the window
>   The one with the waggedy tail."

I remember "Sixteen Tons."

And "Gaston y'a le téléphon qui son."

I remember the scout song: "Over there in the mountains there was an old chalet white walls shingle roof in front of the door a big silver birch."

I remember:

> "Over there in the mountains
>   There was a fat butt
>   A fat butler from the country
>   Who had a pointed end
>   A pointed end-of-the-century look
>   That made his mistress hot"
> (hotel?)

〰 429 〰

I remember: I'm fed up, up to nothing, nothing to do,
do it yourself, self's the man, man of the house, house of
Windsor, Windsor knot, not at home, home and away,
away you go, go to hell, etc.

〰 430 〰

I remember how much I liked Johan Strauss, and how
happy I was when I saw "Viennese Waltzes" at Châtelet.

〰 431 〰

I remember that the word RADAR is an acronym; and also
the word NYLON which concealed an insulting allusion to
the Japanese (because of artificial silk); I remember rayon.

〰 432 〰

I remember an advert in verse which ended like this
(I've forgotten the start of the first line):

> "… his face's page,
> The wrinkles on his brow like mountain passes,
> But his eyes have fought off the onslaught of age,
> Thanks to STIGMAL lenses and HORIZON glasses."

〰 433 〰

I remember a radio program called *La Famille Duraton*.

〰 434 〰

I remember Davy Crockett fur hats.

I remember when I used to go and fetch milk in a battered tin can.

I remember *From Here to Eternity*.

I remember having won a canasta tournament.

I remember Mijanou Bardot.

I remember Ephraim Zimbalist.

I remember:

> "Today's your birthday party, father dear,
> Mummy told me you wouldn't be around.
> I bought some flowers to put in your hair …"
> (I've forgotten the rest).

I remember:

> "We're not complete and utter fools,
>   Some of us even grow wise,
>   At the school of butt
>   At the school of butt
>   At the school of butterflies."

≈ 442 ≈

I remember the racing cyclists Emile Idée and Guy Lapébie.

≈ 443 ≈

I remember hula hoops.

≈ 444 ≈

I remember yo-yos.

≈ 445 ≈

I remember the film *Sissy* with Romy Schneider.

≈ 446 ≈

I remember *Farrebique.*

≈ 447 ≈

I remember *I like Ike* and US GO HOME and Barry Goldwater (AuH_2O).

I remember the café owned by the cyclist Jean Robic, on Avenue du Maine.

I remember Jean Yanne's comedy programs on Radio-Luxembourg, and his unforgettable puns: Don't shoot, I'm on the wagon! This is billion dollar abbot! Nine actors mull to play by two! The gullible bee leaves parliament! etc.

I remember several athletes: Houvion, Thiam Papa Gallo, Sainte-Rose, Jazy, Piquemal, Pujazon, and also Valeri Brumell (who was in a terrible car crash), and Ter Ovanessian.

I remember Robert Mitchum when he says "Children…" in the film *The Night of the Hunter* by Charles Laughton.

I remember the three ways of attaching skis, in the hollow of the heel, with a cable stretched in front of the foot, and with straps.

I remember:

- What color do you see when you look at a pea?
- Green.
- Better see a doctor, then. Pee's yellow.

I remember *Branquignol*, and *Dugudu*, and *Ah les belles Bacchantes.*

I remember Frank Fernandel.

I remember the little firecrackers wrapped in paper that were known as Algerian bombs.

I remember Émilie Allais, and James Couttet, and Henri Oreiller.

I remember Gloria Lasso, and Tilda Thamar, and Maria Felix.

I remember the Point du Jour property scandal, and the Garantie foncière scam, etc., etc., etc.

I remember the duel between the Marquis of Cuevas and Serge Lifar.

✎ 461 ✎

I remember newsreels at the cinema.

✎ 462 ✎

I remember the second hand bookshops there used to be
under the colonnade of the Odéon.

✎ 463 ✎

I remember "Balzac, Helder, Scala, Vivienne."

✎ 464 ✎

I remember the ladies who darned stockings on their little
machines in kiosks at the entrance of department stores.

✎ 465 ✎

I remember Yma Sumac (the nightingale of the Andes).

✎ 466 ✎

I remember Doctor Schweitzer.

✎ 467 ✎

I remember René-Louis Lafforgue singing "Julie la Rousse."

✎ 468 ✎

I remember that buses used to be identified by letters and
not by numbers (hence the celebrated "S" bus of Queneau's
Exercises in Style, now the 84).

I remember Brigitte Bardot singing, but I can't remember whether it was "Sidonie a plus d'un amant," "Moi je ne crains personne en Harley-Davidson," or "La fin de l'été."

I remember *The Egg and I* by Betty McDonald.

I remember American cars: De Sotos, Studebakers, Pontiacs, Oldsmobiles, Chevrolets, Packards, and V8s, so called because they had eight cylinders arranged in a V.

I remember *The Notebooks of Major Thomson*.

I remember *How to be an Alien* and *How to Scrape Skies*, by George Mikes.

I remember *Dear Caroline* (the book and the film).

I remember "usable square footage."

I remember "displaced persons."

꒰ 477 ꒱

I remember that the métro line Nord-Sud didn't have exactly the same carriages as the others.

꒰ 478 ꒱

I remember

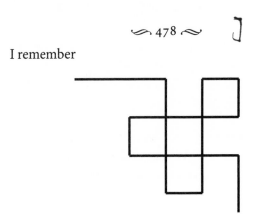

in the métro.

꒰ 479 ꒱

I remember the courageous captain of the Flying Enterprise.

꒰ 480 ꒱

I remember...

(to be continued ...)

Postscript

These I remembers, *of which a number were published in*
les Cahiers du Chemin *(no. 26, January 1976) were put
together between January 1973 and June 1977. The principle
is straightforward: to attempt to unearth a memory that is
almost forgotten, inessential, banal, common, if not to everyone, at least to many.*

*These memories for the most part belong to the period
when I was between 10 and 25, that is between 1946 and
1961. When I evoke memories from before the war, they
refer for me to a period belonging to the realm of myth:
this explains how a memory can be "objectively" false: for
example, in* I remember *no. 101,* I remember *correctly the
celebrated "Musketeers" of tennis, but of the four names I cite,
only two belong there (Borota and Cochet), Brugnon and
Lacoste having been replaced by Petra and Destremeau who
only became champions much later.*

NOTE 2

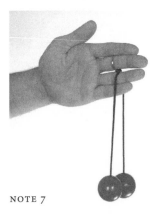

NOTE 7

Notes

The numbers refer to the entries, not to page numbers

2. Perec's uncle, the husband of his father's sister Esther, was a prosperous trader in natural pearls. His car, also mentioned in *W or The Memory of Childhood*, p. 157, was the famous Citroën 11CV—the emblematic black sedan used by French police from the 1930s to the 1950s. During WWII the Gestapo and the Free French also drove 11CVs; after the war, the model became the vehicle of choice for French gangsters, Australian taxi-drivers, and, much later on, for me. GB registration plate KYF 493D, where are you now?

5. The "red lantern" is the rider who comes in last in a cycle stage race.

7. Clackers, also called Ker-Bangers, consist of two plastic spheres suspended on string, to be swung up and down so as to bang against each other, making a clacking sound. They are formed out of two hard plastic balls, each about 5 cm in diameter attached to a tab with a sturdy string.

8. David Howard was his name. See *A Life in Words*, p. 116.

9. The jingle of a phone-in radio show, *On chante dans notre quartier*.

10. On cousin Henri, see *W or The Memory of Childhood*, p. 75

12. *Barbu* is a card game, also known as *kong*. On Les Petites-Dalles, see *A Life in Words*, p. 302

13. The Three Sees were French-speaking enclaves inside the German-speaking Holy Roman Empire until 1522; thereafter they were governed by France and formally incorporated by the Treaty of Westphalia in 1648.

14. Bread was yellow owing to the use of imported corn flour to make up for the shortage of French-grown wheat.

15. The anonymous addressee of Perec's second-person novel, *A Man Asleep*, spends a lot of time at pinball machines.

16. *L'Illustration*, founded in 1843, was the oldest illustrated weekly in France. It was closed down in 1944, for political reasons.

19. The opening of Heine's *Die Lorelei* is remembered at slightly greater length (and with slightly greater accuracy) in "53 *Days*," p. 17.

21. The opening credit of a daily 5-minute radio broadcast of sheer nonsense that ran from 1956 to 1960. "Amédée," under his real name (see Index), later perpetrated a magnificent hoax by forging medieval parchments which, once plagiarized and then translated, provided Dan Brown with the main elements of *The Da Vinci Code*. *Signé Furax* was a similarly comical radio serial of the same period.

22. See *IR* 10

27. Until 1967, the Tour de France (which Bobet won in 1953, 1954 and 1955) finished at the Parc des Princes stadium, right next to Lycée Claude-Bernard, Perec's secondary school.

29. A verse epic from the thirteenth century and a narrative in prose from the late fifteenth century, respectively.

31. This cousin is Ela Bienenfeld, born 1927.

32. Perec's index has an entry for Duke of Edinburgh, with a reference to this item. In fact, Mountbatten was the name of the Duke of Edinburgh's uncle Louis, the last Viceroy of India. Lord Mountbatten of Burma was assassinated by the IRA in 1979.

33. A similar memory in *W or The Memory of Childhood*, p. 135.

35. Marcel Cerdan, world-champion middleweight and lover of Edith Piaf, never did fight Laurent Dauthuille.

36. "Pescade" and "Matifou" are also the names of two acrobats in Jules Verne's *Mathias Sandorf*.

37. De Larminat came out of retirement in 1961 to serve as judge in the trial of the four generals who had led the Algiers Putsch (*IR* 217). He committed suicide before the sentencing began.

40. September 2, 1945. In *W or The Memory of Childhood*, p. 150, Perec records the same memory, but places it at a different date.

43. First published in 1958 and almost certainly the work of a

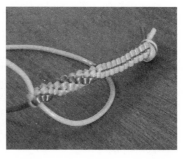

NOTE 51 NOTE 62

twentieth-century musicologist, the piece known as Albinoni's
Adagio in G Minor provided the musical theme for Orson Welles's
film of Kafka's *The Trial* (1962).

45. Félix Gaffiot's *Illustrated Latin–French Dictionary* was an indis-
pensible resource for all school students from the 1930s until the
1970s, when the teaching of Latin was cut back. In his schooldays
the narrator of "*53 Days*" often had to conjugate twenty times
over "in every person, tense, and mood, 'I do not copy out without understanding them sentences of Virgil given as examples in
Gaffiot'" (p. 14).

50. Sacha Distel ran the school band at Lycée Claude-Bernard from
1948. See the note to IR 27 above.

51. First introduced in the 1930s, buses with open rear decks were
still common in Paris in the early 1960s. They were phased out
between 1965 and 1970; the last one ran on Line 21 on 23
January 1971.

55. "Eleska" is a brand of drinking cocoa. The slogan was a clever
play on the names of the letters in French, and right up Perec's
street: *Le KKO LSK est Xki*, "*le cacao Eleska est exquis*".

62. A scoubidou, also called a gimp, lanyard, scoubi, scoobie, boon-
doggle, poopy loopy, or rex-lace is a plaited string loop. It was a
fad in France in the late 1950s and has remained popular among
children. The name "Scoubidou" comes from Sacha Distel's first
hit song, recorded in 1958. See IR 50.

63. Dopal, the first hair hygiene product to be marketed in France, was invented in 1908 and was marketed in liquid form as Dop from 1935. At that time French people washed their hair on average twice a year. The "Dop, dop, dop" jingle was used as part of a public hygiene campaign in the 1930s and it featured frequently in children's movies in the 1950s.

64. *Le Hérisson* ("The Hedgehog") was a satirical weekly launched in 1946. No trace has been found of the boxing matches Perec remembers.

66. The Frères Jacques was a barber-shop quartet whose parody of the theme of the first movement of Beethoven's Fifth Symphony, *La Pince à Linge* ("The Clothes-Peg") still brings tears to my eyes. It features a device for removing the seeds from gooseberries.

69. See *W or The Memory of Childhood*, p. 88.

73. The Drugstore Saint-Germain, which opened in 1965, was not a drug store but a swish bar-cum-brasserie for the beautiful people. I don't think I would have been allowed in.

74. A vaguely cubist logo for a large department store.

75. A regular one-minute radio broadcast protesting an administrative snafu or an act of brutality.

76. Motor-paced cycle racing is a very dangerous sport and was finally dropped from the International Cycling Union's list of recognized events in 1994. From the 1920s to the 1950s, however, it provided major spectacles in velodromes and open-air stadiums, with endurance events lasting six days (yes, six days!) and speed challenges that reached nearly 80 kph. For more details as well as a gripping yarn on the subject, see "The Tale of the Saddler, his Sister and her Mate" on pp. 395–405 of *Life A User's Manual*.

79. General Mathew B. Ridgway (1895–1993) headed the UN force in the Korean War (1950–1953). Black propaganda orchestrated by the Soviet Union persuaded many people in France that he had used bacteriological weapons, and there were mass protests on the occasion of Ridgway's visit to Paris in 1952. He subsequently became Supreme Allied Commander of NATO and

NOTE 76

then Chief of Staff of the US Army. See Romain Gary's Goncourt Prize-winning novel, *The Roots of Heaven* (1956), for a reasonably accurate sidelight on the germ-warfare allegations.

81. Perec lived in and near Villard-de-Lans, near Grenoble, from 1942 to 1945.

82. A 1950 hit song by Robert Lamoureux. Also the theme song of a film by the same title made in 1955.

85. Viktor Kravchenko was a Soviet diplomat who defected to the USA and published the first full-length account of the Moscow show trials of the 1930s and of the Soviet gulag system, *I Chose Freedom* (1946). The cultural organ of the French Communist Party, *Les Lettres Françaises*, claimed that Kravchenko was an illiterate drunk whose book had been entirely fabricated by the CIA. Kravchenko sued for libel in the French courts—and won. Damages were set at 1 franc.

88. The French sentence has the literal (and irrelevant) meaning "A mercenary soldier lives by murky pillage alone." It is the solution to a classic schoolboy's picture-riddle, or rebus, that uses no less than six vulgar synonyms for "penis" (*dard, nœud, vit, queue, pine, zob*) plus two rats, one numeral, and a closing literal.

90. The names of two cafés on the corner of Rue Soufflot and Boulevard Saint-Michel, near the Sorbonne.

91. Here's the cover design:

NOTE 91

92. *Quatre-quarts* has no milk in it, but it does contain eggs. The other ingredients listed are correct.

93. Four out of the five historic French trading posts on the Indian subcontinent. The other one was Chandernagor (now known as Chandannagar).

95. Further adventures of Gromeck are to be found in *Life A User's Manual*, pp. 182, 183.

97. Yves Coudé du Foresto occupied many senior government positions in his long career, but never that of delegate to the UN.

101. The "four musketeers" of French tennis who dominated the Davis Cup from 1927 to 1932 were Jean Borotra, Jacques Brugnon, Henri Cochet, and René Lacoste. Perec got the names right in *Life A User's Manual*, p. 222.

104. René Kovacs was the organizer of a bazooka attack on a military building in Algiers on January 16, 1957, one of the first outrages committed against French institutions by right-wing activists seeking to "keep Algeria French." Kovacs was never caught and was sentenced to death *in absentia*.

105. "Bébé Cadum" was the brand image of a make of soap. Though it changed over time and included bare buttocks in the 1970s, the image Perec remembered must have been something like this:

NOTE 105

111. From 1960 to 1964, on two routes only: from Bourse to Porte Maillot, and from Invalides to Place Clichy.

114. A song sung by Maurice Chevalier, first performed in 1935.

118. Yves Klein, inventor of "International Klein Blue," had his first one-man show in 1955 and another exhibition in the Allendy Gallery in 1956. Rue de l'Assomption is where Perec lived (in the apartment of his aunt Esther and her husband David Bienenfeld) from 1945 to 1956.

124. An Italian liner that collided with the S.S. Stockholm just outside New York harbor on July 25, 1956. It was the worst civilian maritime disaster since the sinking of the Titanic.

135. And I remember that Henri Salvador has the most infectious and life-enhancing laugh I have ever heard.

137. On April 12, 1960, four-year-old Éric Peugeot was kidnapped. He was the great-grandson of the founder of the Peugeot automobile firm, and a ransom of 50 million (old) francs was paid for his release.

151. Louise de Vilmorin was a novelist related to the owners of Les Établissements Vilmorin, France's principal retail distributor of seeds.

155. Philippe Pétain, an old soldier, was granted authority by the French parliament to negotiate an armistice with Nazi Germany after the invasion of May–June 1940. He became head of the puppet French state based at Vichy that was swept away on the liberation of France in the summer of 1944. He was tried and convicted of treason, but most of his supporters and henchmen, called Pétainistes, were gradually allowed to re-enter public life in the post-war period.

157. Darry Cowl was a music-hall artist who specialized in comical language-mangling. His résumé of Victor Hugo's masterpiece in Claude Lelouch's screen adaptation of *Les Misérables* is one of the greatest treasures to be had from learning French.

167. The FLN, or *Front de Libération Nationale,* was the main organization fighting for the independence of Algeria from 1954 to 1962.

170. The names mean "Two Asses" and "Three Donkeys."

179. The novelist François Mauriac was a Catholic, André Gide not.

182. Marina Vlady, who was of Russian descent, later married the stupendous balladeer Vladimir Vizotsky. Perec got to meet her several times toward the end of his life. Marina Vlady has now published a memoir of Catherine Binet, Perec's companion. See also IR 196. The film's real title was *Before the Deluge.* Perec seems to have muddled it up with a remark allegedly made by Louis XV, "*Après moi, le deluge.*"

197. Minou Drouet was a child prodigy whose poetic talent was disputed by, among others, Jean Cocteau: *Tous les enfants de neuf*

ans ont du génie, sauf Minou Drouet, "All nine-year-olds are
geniuses, except Minou Drouet" (in an article in *Elle* magazine,
12 December, 1955).

199. The scandal, which broke in January 1959, involved underage
sex. Le Troquer was tried and convicted for *outrage aux mœurs*,
roughly "immoral behavior".

205. In 1972 the satirical weekly *Le Canard enchaîné* published facsim-
iles of the (leaked) tax returns of the then Prime Minister, Jacques
Chaban-Delmas. The documents showed that by exploiting legal
loopholes he paid no income tax at all between 1967 and 1970.
This memory is uncharacteristically recent for *I Remember*, and
also, in 2013, strangely familiar.

207. Punning on the names of Charles Trenet, Pierre Fresnay, and
Sophie Desmarets. See the Index for further details.

208. From 1947 to 1968 *Les Lettres Françaises* was the cultural mouth-
piece of the French Communist Party. It closed in 1972.

214. They were found in the trunk of his car on the night before the
Ridgway demonstration (see the note to IR 79). As Duclos was
a leading Communist politician he was arrested on suspicion of
being in possession of secret communications equipment. However, the birds turned out not to be carrier pigeons, just the main
ingredient of Duclos's (much-delayed) dinner.

217. The Algiers Putsch of 1961 (see IR 37) was an attempt to wrest
control of French policy in Algeria from de Gaulle. The four generals were arrested and imprisoned but released in 1968 under
a general amnesty and restored to their military ranks by President Mitterrand in 1982. The obsolete word that de Gaulle used
to denigrate them—*quarteron*, meaning "handful" but also "a
fourth part" as well as "quadroon"—proved to be a highly effec-
tive put-down, possibly because few people knew what it meant.

229. The play, put on in 1951, was a polemic against the Korean War.
Right-wing protesters broke up the first two performances with
great violence, and the Interior Ministry banned the play in the
name of public order.

230: Landru and Petiot were both serial killers who dismembered and then incinerated their victims. Landru was guillotined in 1922, Petiot in 1946.

231. A television program. Perec never owned a set.

237. The Drugstore des Champs-Elysées, the first in France, opened in 1957 and burned down in 1972. See also the note on IR 205.

241. In 1962, Bombard broke the world record for staying alive on an inflatable dinghy by paddling his way from Tangiers to Barbados.

243. In 1960 one hundred and twenty-one intellectuals signed a manifesto drafted by Maurice Blanchot and edited by Dionys Mascolo asserting the right of conscripts to disobey orders and to evade military service in Algeria.

245. An annual competition for amateur inventors.

248. Robert and Gérald Finaly were orphaned Jewish infants who were taken care of by a devout Catholic woman during the German Occupation. After the war, she refused to surrender them to their surviving relatives, as the children were now baptized. Parts of the Catholic hierarchy supported her and even hid the children in a monastery in Spain to prevent their return. The affair became national news and dragged on until 1953, when the children were finally allowed to emigrate to Israel.

250. On August 22, 1962, the OAS, the military wing of the rearguard faction supporting French Algeria (which no longer existed, in fact) ambushed de Gaulle's car as it sped through a traffic junction on the outskirts of Paris. The president was not hurt: he owed his survival to the bravery of his driver and to the hydrolastic suspension of the Citroën limousine he was in.

262. As well he might, because he was a student at the school where Gracq was one of the history teachers.

270. Alain Delon's personal bodyguard was found dead in a landfill site in October 1968. Persistent rumors linked the wife of Georges Pompidou, then Prime Minister, to the murder. The case was never solved.

277. In 1972 industrial waste from a titanium oxide plant on the Italian coast washed on to beaches in Corsica, covering them with

a sludge known as "red mud." The oil tanker Torrey Canyon ran aground on rocks off the Scilly Isles (the most south-westerly part of the United Kingdom) in March 1967, releasing 120,000 tons of crude, much of which drifted onto the coast of Brittany. UK Prime Minister Harold Wilson ordered the RAF to bomb the wreck, sending it and its remaining load to the bottom of the Atlantic, where it now lies.

292. The "Seven Bridges of Königsberg" is a historically notable problem in mathematics. Its negative resolution by Leonhard Euler in 1735 laid the foundations of graph theory and prefigured the idea of topology. The four-color map theorem states that given any separation of a plane into contiguous regions, producing a figure called a *map*, no more than four colors are required to color the regions of the map so that no two adjacent regions have the same color.

298. A gang of bank robbers in the immediate post-war years who drove souped-up Citroën 11cvs, which were front-wheel drive vehicles. See the note on *IR* 2.

303. It means "without a break."

311. The French original recalls three classic schoolboy puns on invented foreign-sounding names: "Ivan Labibine Osouzoff," *il vend la bibine aux sous-off* ("he sells booze to the NCO");

"Yamamoto Kakapoté," *il y a ma moto qu'a capoté* ("now my motorbike has broken down"); and "Harry Cover," *haricots verts* ("string beans").

314. Wakouwas were articulated, spring-loaded puppet toys made of wood. The original was a dog, but many other designs existed (giraffes, monkeys, etc.).

319. A tube-shaped chocolate bar in a cellophane twist.

320. Also recalled in *Life A User's Manual*, p. 69.

321. Perec was a boarder at the Collège Geoffroy Saint-Hilaire at Étampes in three of his secondary school years. His experiences there form the basis of pp. 14–21 of his unfinished detective novel, "*53 Days*".

324. A classic tale of mountaineering first published in 1941 and adapted for the screen in 1944.

331. The address is 29, Rue Jussieu. It's odd that Perec gets the street name wrong (he writes Rue de Jussieu), seeing as he lived round the corner (first in Rue de Quatrefages, then in Rue Linné) for a large part of his adult life. The theater closed in 1969.

333. Tag name for the *Rote Armee Fraktion*, a left-wing terrorist group that committed at least four murders in West Germany between 1970 and 1977.

337. Hardly anybody else remembers the man. He was a distinguished, long-serving French politician often mocked as having all the dash and wit of a dairy cow. The subject of a caricature with a five-star caption: *le meuh est l'ennemi du bien.* Understanding this quip is the second most valuable treasure to be gained from learning French.

338. The slogan of a campaign to moderate food price inflation in 1960.

345. *Furax* also crops up in IR 21. See the note.

351. A famous and long-running legal mystery. Marie Besnard was accused of poisoning twelve of her close relatives with arsenic over a period of twenty years. She denied everything. After a series of trials beginning in 1949 she was finally acquitted of all charges in 1961.

361. *Bach-Werke-Verzeichnis,* the index of the musical works of Johann Sebastian Bach.

366. The Holy Vase was seized by the Frankish king Clovis after he trounced Syagrius at the Battle of Soissons in 486 CE. The mythical origin of the French nation.

367. These were motorized three-wheel bubble cars invented in Italy but mostly manufactured by BMW in the 1950s. Cheap and nasty.

NOTE 367

370. Abbé Pierre campaigned tirelessly on behalf of the homeless, collecting funds through charity shops. The project and the shops have now spread to other countries, under the name Emmaüs.

374. Emil Zatopek won the marathon at the 1952 Helsinki Olympics. He inspired millions to take up cross-country running. Even me. ⟩

377. Honking has been illegal in Paris since 1954.

381. Reginald Harris, an Olympic gold medalist, held several world speed records for many years. He made a heart-warming comeback in the 1970s by winning the British Road Championship at the age of 54. My hero.

383. A political campaigner opposed both to the French Communist party *and* to Algerian independence.

393. This memory is exceedingly murky. See *W or The Memory of Childhood*, pp 54–55 and 79–80 for further complications.

395. The advertising slogan for chocolate-coated peanuts marketed as Treets.

397. A dance hall and a music hall, respectively.

399. Jolly Dutch anarchists who organized "happenings" in Amsterdam in the 1960s. Nothing to do with the Provisional IRA.

407. These are long-standing schoolboy macaronics. The first is in kitchen Greek, but it just about makes sense in both Greek and French. The second makes no sense in Latin but when pronounced in French it says "Caesar likes cream and rum buns." A good pronunciation exercise for foreign-language learners of French.

408. Yes, there really is a cycle race from Paris to Camembert.

410. Demolished in 1965. The current Gare Montparnasse dates from 1969. For the reasons why the old station was demolished and replaced in part by the enormously high Maine-Montparnasse Tower, see the closing pages of Frederick Forsyth's *Day of the Jackal*.

412. Respectively the director of the Tour de France and a sports journalist.

418. A Renault sedan designed in the 1930s but still in production in the post-war period.

NOTE 418   NOTE 443

420. Meccano, invented by the British engineer Frank Hornby, is the
     original name of an educational toy marketed in the US as Erec-
     tor Sets, now manufactured by a Japanese company in France and
     China.
431. RADAR stands for **Ra**dio **D**etecting **a**nd **R**anging. The origin of
     the word nylon is obscure, but the explanation that Perec alludes
     to—"**N**ow, **Y**ou **L**ousy **O**ld **N**ipponese"—must be apocryphal.
432. See *Thoughts of Sorts*, p. 116, for an alternative version of this
     jingle.
443. A hip-swinging plastic toy derived from ancient popular enter-
     tainments, launched by Arthur K. Melin and Richard Knerr in
     1958 under a name allegedly borrowed from Hawaiian. It soon
     became a world-wide craze.
444. So do I.
446. An almost anthropological documentary film that chronicles
     a year in the life of a family of farmers in a remote part of Au-
     vergne. Made by Georges Rouquié, released in 1947. A must-see.
454. Three comedy shows put on by Robert Dhéry in 1948, 1951, and
     1953 respectively.
455. Son of Fernandel, the comedian with the mile-wide smile.
459. Spectacular real-estate swindles that became news in 1957 and
     1971 respectively.

460. A professional disagreement between these two distinguished
   ballet-masters was settled by a sword-fight in March 1958.
   Cuevas's second was Jean-Marie Le Pen. Lifar got a scratch and
   conceded.

463. Between 1949 and 1965 these four Paris cinemas ran the same
   programs. What Perec means to record here is the sonorous
   voice-over that came at the end of trailers for coming attractions
   in any one of the cinemas.

471. The French passion for oversize US-made automobiles is chroni-
   cled by Kristin Ross in *Fast Cars, Clean Bodies* (MIT Press, 1995).
   A different approach can be enjoyed in Robert Dhéry's *La Belle
   Américaine* (1961), starring the lovably vulgar Louis de Funès.

472. An affectionate satire of French foibles by Pierre Daninos,
   published in 1954. It's Perec who spelled the Major's name
   incorrectly.

474. A historical romance by Cecil Saint-Laurent, published in 1947.

475. The French term, *surface corrigée*, is mildly amusing.

476. In the aftermath of WWII the Allies distinguished between refugees, people stranded away from their place of abode in their home countries, and displaced persons (DPs), stranded abroad. DPs were issued travel documents drafted by the novelist Albert Cohen, who considered the wording to be his greatest contribution to world literature.

478. The design was used as a corner decoration on several types of signage on the Paris metro. Roland Brasseur points out that you can extract a swastika from it.

479. A Danish captain, Kurt Carlsen, who was the last to leave his sinking ship in foul weather in January 1952. MV Flying Enterprise was transporting zirconium to a nuclear submarine.

NOTE 478

Index

Numbers refer to the numbers of the I remembers.

At the request of the author a number of blank pages have been left at the end for readers to write their own "I remembers" which the reading of these ones will hopefully have inspired.

A NOTE ON THE TYPE

THE TEXT OF THIS BOOK was set in Minion, a word that
not only refers to a size of type but also is defined as "faithful
companion." Minion was designed by Robert Slimbach for
Adobe Systems in 1990. In Slimbach's own words,

> I like to think of Minion as a synthesis of historical and
> contemporary elements. My intention with the design was
> to make a progressive Aldine style text family that is both
> stylistically distinctive and utilitarian. The design grew
> out of my formal calligraphy, written in the Aldine style.
> By adapting my hand lettering to the practical concerns
> of computer aided text typeface design, I hoped to design
> a fresh interpretation of a classical alphabet.

DESIGN & COMPOSITION BY MICHAEL RUSSEM AT KAT RAN PRESS